Wher the Wind?

Written by Celia Warren

Illustrated by Lisa Williams

Collins

Mole said,
"I'm going to see the wind."

2

3

Mole said,
"Hello, Bee. Did you see the wind?"
Bee said, "No."

Mole said,
"Hello, Mouse. Did you see the wind?"
Mouse said, "No."

7

Mole said,
"Hello, Deer. Did you see the wind?"
Deer said, "No."

8

Mole said,
"Hello, Toad. Did you see the wind?"
Toad said, "No."

Mum said, "Did you see the wind?"
Mole said, "No. It wasn't there!"

Mole looks for the wind

Ideas for guided reading

Curriculum links: Knowledge and understanding of the world: finding out about features of living things, objects and events.

Learning objectives: Tracking text in the right order; pointing while reading; making one-to-one correspondences between written and spoken words; expecting written text to make sense and checking for sense if it does not; phoneme-grapheme correspondences; interacting with others, negotiating plans and taking turns in conversation

Interest words: mole, going, see, wind, bee, hello, mouse, deer, toad, wasn't, there, looks, I'm, did

High frequency words: the, said, to, you, no, it, mum

Word count: 69

Getting started

- Hide the word *wind* and show the children the front cover. Explain that this is a story about Mole who is looking for something, and ask the children to predict what it is from the cover image. Reveal the initial letter *w* if necessary.

- Ask the children in pairs to discuss where they could find the wind – is it possible to catch the wind?

- Turn to pp2-3, model pointing and one-to-one matching accurately, and use expression when reading text inside speech marks. Ask the children to read these pages, and praise accurate pointing and expression.

- Walk through the story up to p13 discussing what happens in the pictures.

Reading and responding

- Ask the children to read the story independently and aloud at their own pace to p13, making sure that they point to each word as they read it. Encourage the children to attempt all unknown words using initial sounds and picture cues. Check that the children maintain accuracy as they become familiar with the pattern of the sentences.

- As they read, encourage children to predict the ending, e.g. *Will Mole find the wind? Why/why not?*